WE'RE GOING SOMEPLACE SPECIAL...

LET'S INVITE OUR FRIENDS!

FOR RENFIELD

Copyright © 2011 Aron Nels Steinke

Balloon Toons® is a registered
trademark of Harriet Ziefert, Inc.
All rights reserved/CIP data is available.
Published in the United States 2011 by

🍎 Blue Apple Books

515 Valley Street, Maplewood, NJ 07040

www.blueapplebooks.com

First Edition 08/11
Printed in China

HC ISBN: 978-1-60905-093-1
2 4 6 8 10 9 7 5 3 1
PB ISBN: 978-1-60905-184-6
2 4 6 8 10 9 7 5 3 1

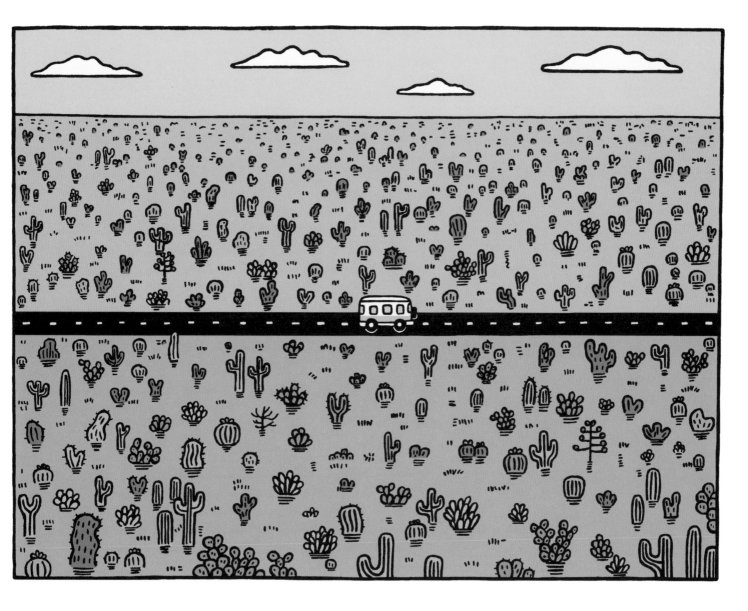

TO DOG BEACH

SPACE DOG MEMORIAL SKATE PARK